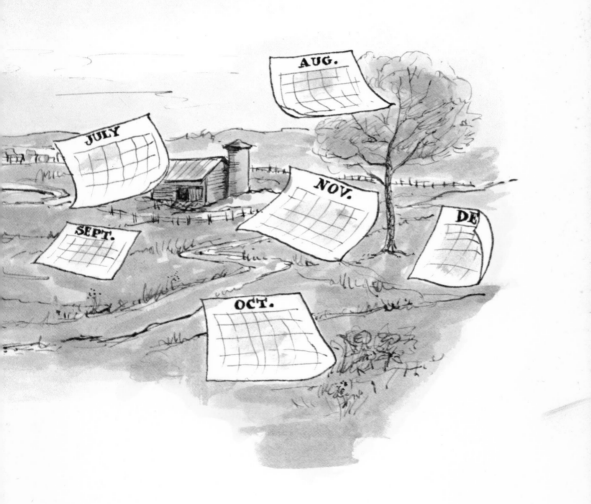

Grandma's Holidays

*(Some are known, and some are not,
For some the calendar forgot.)*

By Doris Adelberg

Illustrated by Paul Kennedy

THE DIAL PRESS NEW YORK

For Lotte

MANUFACTURED IN THE UNITED STATES OF AMERICA

On New Year's Eve, in our town,
All the grownups grow back down—
Mothers, fathers, uncles, aunts,
Even grandmas, sing and dance,
Wear hats, blow horns, make lots of noise,
And act like little girls and boys—
Except *my* grandma. She's with me.
We spend this evening quietly,
Staying up till very late,
And whispering how we'll celebrate,
In certain very special ways,
Grandma's favorite holidays.

64093

New Year's Day

Last night—oh no, I mean last year,
My grandma said she'd bring me here,
Up to the top of this high hill,
Where everything is bright, and still,
And new, the day the year is new.
And here we are, alone, us two—
Grandma and I, out in the snow,
Making footprints where we go,
Grandma and I, up with the sun,
To meet the year that has begun.

Valentine Day

Grandmas bring candy on this day,
Or send a card, if they're away,
With hearts and lace and "I love you."
That's what most people's grandmas do.
But not *my* grandma. Look what mine
Brought me for a Valentine:

It is scrawny, it can purr,
It has a grayish-whitish fur,
Two green eyes, one heart-shaped note
On a string around its throat:
"Here's a little cat I found,
To love you, dear, the whole year round."

Bird-Helping Day

Last fall, the songbirds flew away,
To find a warmer place to stay.
How long we've longed to hear them sing!
But they'll be back now that it's spring,
And Grandma says, we ought to try
To help them with their nests. That's why,
Dressed in our dungarees,
We're busy making—out of these
Strips of paper, cotton, string,
Silk and straw—*the strangest thing.*
We hang it from a branch and—hush—
A bird is coming! It's a thrush.
We listen, but he will not sing,
Because his beak is stuffed with string
He pulled out from the thing we made—
Which is a *bird-nest-building-aid!*

Easter

Grandma knows a secret land,
Where rows of Easter lilies stand,
Always blooming, always white,
Where the weather's always right,
And the meadow's always green,
Where nobody has ever been,
Except some shepherd boys who keep
Watching tiny lambs and sheep,
Where I would like to go right now,
And so would you, if you knew how.

You cannot go by railroad train,
By bus, by boat or aeroplane,
By bicycle or car,
But not because it's far—
Because it's just behind a pane
Of ordinary cellophane,
And I can hold the secret land
With all its wonders in my hand!
It's in this wonder-egg, you see,
It's Grandma's Easter gift to me.

Decoration Day

On the thirtieth of May,
Which is Decoration Day,
You should decorate the grave
Of someone who was good and brave.

Well, *I* know someone good and brave—
A dog named Duke, we used to have.
He got old, and then he died,
You can imagine how I cried.
We buried him beneath a tree,
Where he's been resting peacefully.

Beneath that tree, we plant a rose.
Why do we do this? No one knows,
Except for Grandma, and for me:
We plant it there in memory
Of our Duke, so brave, so good,
Who'd love to sniff it, if he could!

River Day

"Get ready, on your mark, get set—"
"Oh Grandma, wait, please, not just yet—"
Grandma's in! And with a shiver,
I also jump into the river.
We kick, we crawl, we have a race,
She splashes water in my face.
We plunge right down, with open eyes,
We watch the golden bubbles rise,
We touch the deep, dark river ground,
And come back up, and swim around
Just like two sweet water trout
Till Grandma says, "Time to come out!"

The air is cool. It's only June,
But never mind, it's not too soon,
I'm not too young, she's not too old,
And we're not going to catch cold!
Without a sniffle or a sneeze, on
River Day we start the season.

Independence Day

America, in days of old,
Was not a country yet, I'm told,
And not yet free, and had to be
Another country's colony.
That was the problem. The solution
Was to have a Revolution.
And we had it. That is why,
On every fourth day of July,
We wave the flag and we make noise,
Which almost everyone enjoys.

The firecrackers bang and boom
While Grandma's sitting in her room.
"Grandma, please come out," I say,
"Because it's Independence Day."
She answers, "It's a day, my dear,
Which I'd prefer to spend right here,
In peace and quiet. Let's agree
To spend it independently!"

Blackberry Day

The sun's still down. The grass is wet.
Not even birds have wakened yet.
But we are up. I have to yawn,
Picking berries before dawn.

"Berries are best while wet with dew.
I'll eat mine now, and so should you,"
Says Grandma. Then we pick some more,
And leave them on the table for
Others to have with sugar and cream,
While we go back to bed to dream.

Learners' Day

"On Labor Day, in all the States,
Everybody celebrates
Those who *labor* and who earn
Their bread with work. But those who *learn,*
Also labor. Let's remember
Learners also, in September."
So I've heard my grandma say,
And so we have a Learners' Day,
With hide-and-seek, and blindman's buff,
Potato races, and enough
Chocolate cake for all those who'll
Soon be going back to school.

Halloween

Once, when I went trick-or-treating,
All wrapped up in snow-white sheeting,
On the spooky, scary evening of the night of Halloween,
A shape in black went creeping near me,
Made the neighbors cry, "Oh dear me!"
What a fright'ning sight! You should have seen
It with its broomstick and its black
Knapsack hanging down its back—
Whatever in the wide world might that strange black shape
  have been?
What was in that sack of black?

Popcorn, nuts and crackerjack,
And for every child an orange, apple, pear or tangerine!

That was no witch, no elf, no sprite,
Out scaring people in the night—
That was just my grandma, having fun on Halloween!

Thanksgiving

We gather together for turkey and yams,
For cranberry sauce and for stuffing with clams.
The holiday table is set for eight.
Seven sit down. My grandma's late.

I wait. I eat. I watch the door.
She doesn't come. I wait some more,
And eat some more. Oh how I miss
My grandma while I eat all this!

And while I eat my pumpkin pie,
I miss her so, I start to cry.
How full I am, how sad I feel,
To think my grandma missed this meal!

Where *is* my grandma? She went out
For frankfurters and sauerkraut.

Grandma's back. She dries my tears.
She says, "My dear, in all these years,
I've had so many, many yams,
And so much turkey stuffed with clams,
So very many cranberries,
That now I eat just what I please.
It doesn't matter what the food,
My heart is full of gratitude.
So I went out and gave my thanks
Over sauerkraut and franks."

Christmas

Till Christmas Eve, in every store,
On the toy department floor,
A fat and bearded Santa Claus
Must smile, and ring his bell, because
Some grandmas take *some* girls and boys
To visit him and look at toys.

Mine refused. She shook her head,
And took me somewhere else instead.

To see the tree in Central Square?
No, Grandma did not take me there.

To watch the shoppers on the go
All over town? The answer's no!

To a play? A Christmas show?
No again! Where *did* we go?

Through the meadow, arm in arm,
To McAttleborough's farm,
To see the donkey, ox and cow.
We've seen them all before, but now,
The while they gently moo and bray,
We see them in a special way,
And almost see those beasts as well,
Who saw the very first Noel.

And One More

The new year's old, and almost done.
All holidays have come but one—
A holiday I think it rude
The calendar did not include.

Is it a second Christmas? No!
Then why these sprigs of mistletoe,
With holly, and with twigs of pine?

They're for a relative of mine—
For though the calendar forgot
All about her, I did not.
And with my wintertime bouquet,
I wish her HAPPY GRANDMA'S DAY!

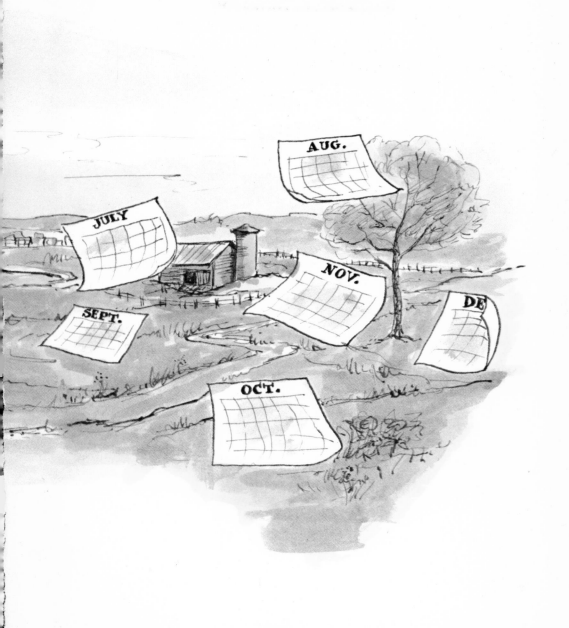